CATS AND CATNAPPING

A MIRA MICHAELS MYSTERY

JULIA KOTY

BUSSTOP PRESS

First paperback edition March 2021

Cover design by Kim Thurlow
Book design by Natasha Sass

ISBN 978-1-939309-21-1 (paperback)
ISBN 978-1-939309-22-8 (large print paperback)
ISBN 978-1- 939309-20-4(ebook)
www.JuliaKoty.com

❀ Created with Vellum

For Heather

CATS AND CATNAPPING

By Julia Koty

1

The chilly spring morning was the perfect backdrop for my getaway. Crisp and clear. I shoved another box into my old Buick's trunk. It wouldn't fit until I forced it in between two other boxes. I didn't even care if everything broke. I needed to escape. The messy bun at the nape of my neck came loose. I tightened the ponytail, twisted it quickly around and tucked the ends of my hair back inside.

"I'm done with men. I'm done with my sister. I need my own life." I laid my grandmother's quilt carefully on top of the boxes and then slammed the trunk lid. I shook my head. No need to be angry with Babs. I patted her gray steel trunk in apology, while saying a prayer to the car gods that my ancient Buick would survive the trip.

"Meow." The sound came from the cat carrier that sat in the shadow of the passenger side door of the Electra.

"Don't you get started. I haven't forgotten about you." I picked up Arnold's carrier and sat him in the passenger seat, running the seatbelt through his carrier handle and into the clip. "We're leaving."

I ducked back out and took one moment to enjoy the

unseasonably warm spring breeze. I loved all of New England's seasons. I tried not to have second thoughts of leaving. After all, Pennsylvania still had all four seasons. In fact, I bet there were already leaves budding on the trees.

My sister's car roared up, forcing me to return to my resolve. She screeched to a halt in the driveway and blocked my car. As expected, trying to control the situation again. Trying to control me. How did she even know I was leaving? Ugh. There was nothing more annoying than a virtuous older sister. A virtuous, *psychic,* older sister. How far away would I need to go to get away from the grip of her psychic vibes? Hopefully her psychic reach ended at the interstate.

Her short glossy curly hair was the first out of the car, then the rest of her petite frame. Just over five feet, Darla had a calm but vibrant energy about her, that people gravitated toward. "Mira, what are you doing?"

"I'm moving out." I opened the back of the car and ran through my mental checklist. As long as I had my phone charger, wallet, and all of Arnold's things, I was fine. I double-checked that all of Arnold's items were within reach. Gallon of water. Water bowl. Cat food. Makeshift litter box. Scooper. I ignored my sister. She was not going to talk me out of this. Psych me out of this? I was tired of the whole big-sister-is-a-psychic excuse that she used to try to run my life.

"I *feel* that this is a bad idea." Darla's voice grew louder as she rounded the car.

"You don't know that." I closed the door and faced my sister.

"I most certainly do. You'll find a great deal of trials if you go this route." Her psychic mumbo jumbo was showing. And I was so done.

"A 'great deal of trials?' Can't you just talk like a sister?

Right now, anything would be better than this." I waved my hands between the two of us.

"What?" She looked hurt.

"This. This. You telling me how to run my life. Always. I'm done. I'm moving out."

"Look. I know you felt betrayed, the way things ended with... your ex. But that doesn't mean the heartache is going to end. In fact, that house is going to give you a lot of problems." She shook her head.

I never should have shown her pictures of my dilapidated investment. You didn't have to be a psychic to see that fixing it up would be trouble. "That's fine. It'll be my heartache. Mine. My new house. My heartache." I pointed to myself like an idiot.

"You're going to do this, aren't you? No matter what I say?"

Had I worn her down? Had her spirit friends reminded her how stubborn I could be?

"The car is packed. Arnold is in the front seat."

"Okay." She opened her arms graciously.

I stared at her. "Okay? That's it?"

"I can't stop you." She frowned.

"I'm going." I stared at her closely.

"Okay."

I waved a finger at her. "Don't call me."

She took a step forward, with a wounded look in her eyes. "Why not?"

"I don't want your advice. I don't want to know what you think the spirits are trying to tell me." I walked around her and opened the car door. "I just want a normal, boring, life."

"But my readings will help you. I just want to help you." Her kindness was what always broke me. I had to be strong.

She meant well. But I needed a new start and a break from her always trying to guide me.

"I don't want your help."

My sister could never be a poker player. She didn't even try to disguise the wounded look on her face.

"Mira, you can't mean that."

"I don't want your help. Don't call me. I'm serious." Anger rose between us like its own entity. I tossed my set of keys at her, and she refused to catch them, letting them clunk to the ground.

"Fine. Be a child." She snapped.

"No. I'm being an adult. For once," I shouted.

I got into the car and slammed the door.

I turned the key in the ignition and said a silent prayer that it would start. I said another prayer of thanks when it did and pulled around Darla and her car. She shouted something about why-at or something, as I pulled away. Away from everything that was holding me back.

Three states and 450 miles to Pennsylvania. Months of planning and now it was actually happening. I resolved to keep Darla and her psychic vibes in my rear-view mirror.

I wasn't about to spend another moment under my sister's thumb. Last year was the worst. Hearing every day about my sister's *feelings* that I was making all the wrong decisions. Trying to fix a bad relationship. Discovering that my boyfriend was a criminal. Watching the police haul him away on television had been the last straw. I put my plan in motion and now I was getting out—starting my own life at last.

I followed the signs to the highway. On my way.

My shoulders relaxed, and I let out a deep breath. I was finally, finally doing this. It felt good, a little scary, but good. And I had my pal, my long-haired black cat, Arnold.

"Partners, right, buddy?" I grinned in the direction of the cat carrier.

I'm inside a locked box. Do I have much choice?

I froze. Not again. I couldn't pretend, even in the privacy of my own mind, that hearing my cat speak inside my head was normal. It had been happening more and more lately and made me feel like a loon. I could block it out, but it took effort. The flip side was also true—I had to pay attention to hear exactly what he was saying. It took effort to hear him clearly and effort to not hear him at all. My cat, talking inside my head. I reminded myself, "I'm not crazy like my sister. I'm not the psychic in the family." I loosened the white-knuckle grip I had on the steering wheel.

"I refuse to be psychic. REFUSE," I shouted to the universe.

I turned on the radio and punched through the stations, finding nothing worth listening to, when the radio glitched out. "No, no, no, I need some sort of music during this 8-hour road trip." I punched the power button a few more times and the LED finally lit up, but without sound. It was obviously too much to ask that my ancient Buick both stay in one piece on the trip and also provide entertainment. I didn't have enough data to stream music on my phone for eight hours. I sighed in exasperation.

I don't want to move to a new territory. I like the house we live in.

My cat's voice rang clear in my head. It took me a long moment to come to a decision. I could either talk to my cat, and just give in to the insanity, or spend eight very long hours bored out of my mind pretending I didn't hear him.

"Fine, Universe, but we have some talking to do about this whole thing." I took a deep, measured breath. "The house we lived in, past tense, is actually under Darla's name and my life is under her thumb, so we're moving out.

Darla says...

"Arnold, I don't care what Darla says..."

That's why that guy wrecked your life, because you refused to listen.

I now second-guessed my decision to listen to my cat. "I'm going to stop listening to you, right now."

"Meow."

"Oh, stop."

Arnold pouted, refusing to meow or talk to me.

The drive across Massachusetts through Connecticut, New York, and then through half of Pennsylvania would be a long one, especially in moody silence. But that was the least of my worries about this car. It was older than the hills. I'd bought it used in high school and it's been with me since. But it had its issues. Like the fact that the rusted-out muffler was held on by some strategically placed coat hanger wire and duct tape. The local auto shop told me that if I didn't replace it before the next inspection, the car wouldn't pass.

I had every intention of fixing the car. Until the guy, who I refuse to give the benefit of a name, ran off with my money. Come to think of it, the name he gave me probably wasn't his own, anyway.

It wasn't.

"What?" I hadn't realized I had said those thoughts about my ex out loud until my cat answered them.

It wasn't his real name. My cat sense told me he was lying.

"Is that why you peed in his shoes?"

Of course.

I laughed. "Thanks.

You know it'll be better for us in the new town. We can make our own decisions."

I always make my own decisions.

I rolled my eyes. My independent cat. "Well, I didn't. Darla always made mine for me."

"Meow," came a snarky vocalization from the carrier.

"What's that supposed to mean?"

You never thought for yourself; you simply did the opposite of whatever Darla told you would be best, and it, most often, was the worst thing you could do.

We sat in silence. At this point, I wished I couldn't hear Arnold. Especially when he was right.

"This change is going to be good for us both." I repeated. Mostly to keep myself from freaking out.

As if on cue, the car backfired, almost giving me a heart attack.

THE REAL CAR trouble started just west of Boston. As if the backfiring had just been a warning shot. The engine light came on and the temperature gauge started to go up. "Crap."

But I knew what this meant. Babs and I had been through a lot since I first got her.

Years ago, in high school, one of my least favorite jobs was waiting tables at the local Italian restaurant. I saved all my tips and put it towards the purchase of this car. Its faded gray paint had once been pearlized and impressive, like a town car. But some formulation error in the topcoat caused it to streak and flake off. The harsh New England winters hadn't helped.

But she always got me from point A to point B. Only this point A and point B were 450 miles apart, a new test for my beloved Buick. I put a hand on the side of the seat and patted the deep maroon velour fabric.

Right now, hopefully all she needed was a new can of oil, and I always kept a case in the back seat.

We just had to find a service station, in case oil wasn't enough, and soon.

"Meow."

"Have a nice nap?"

A catnap is a wonderful way to pass the time. Especially when you're on a long car trip that you don't want to be on like this one.

"The car needs a can of oil, so I need to find a gas station soon. I should top off the tank, anyway. Do you need to use the litter box?"

That's a very personal question.

"I don't want to have to clean out your carrier."

I will let you know if I need some private time with the sandbox.

"Are you hungry? These corn chips aren't cutting it." I pushed the bag away, picked up my water bottle, and took a swig. "Let's see what we can find."

I grabbed my cell phone from off the passenger seat where it leaned against Arnold's carrier. The screen showed the trip's map. I hit search and the gas station icon. There was a gas station a few miles up the road.

"Good. It shouldn't take too long before we get there."

How much farther until we get to this supposed "house"?

"About 400 more miles."

The crying meow that Arnold let out pierced the air and was so agonizing that for a second I wondered if he had hurt himself.

"Stop that." He could be so annoying.

I think I'm going to be sick.

"You are not going to be sick." But then I thought better of my comment. "Do you want some water?"

No. I don't want any water. Why are you making me do this?

"I could have left you with Darla, you know."

Silence.

"Did you want me to leave you with Darla?" I felt horrible. If he didn't want to hang out with me, he could just tell me.

You're my human. I have to stay with you. He paused for a short moment. *I want to stay with you.* I heard him move around inside the carrier. *Besides, I can't stay with Darla, her cats are weird.*

"I'm glad at least I have one up on a set of weird cats."

But why are you making me do this? I hate car rides and I hate new places.

"Trust me. This will be good for both of us. I'll be able to flip the house and make some money and then we can move wherever we want."

Don't you need that imaginary stuff, money, to flip a house? And didn't that male that you shared your territory with take all of your money?

"Yes, well, I'll need to get a job and we'll use that money to fix up the house. I have a plan." I wasn't sure what that was, yet. Right now, the plan was to fix up the house, sell it, and move somewhere else. Maybe flip another house until I can make a decent living.

I pulled onto the next exit ramp, heading to the gas station.

"Oh, here we are." I quickly changed the subject to avoid discussing any more details about what would happen once we got to Pleasant Pond, Pennsylvania.

The trees lining the road were still skeletal, no green signs of leaves yet, and there wasn't much else just off the exit.

"Almost there, girl. I'll get you a new can of oil." I patted and rubbed my hand across the dashboard, not unlike rubbing a talisman for good luck.

The first thing I noticed as we pulled into the gas station was the lack of restaurants nearby. Not even fast food.

Priorities first. Babs needed oil. I pulled into a parking area next to the building. A bottle of 5W-30 oil would fix the problem. I popped the lid to the hood and walked around to the front of the car, putting the bottle of oil on the ground. Lifting this hood was a two-hand job. With one finger I reached under and released the catch and tensed up my abs in preparation to lift the huge piece of metal that served as engine protector for my dilapidated beauty. With one hand holding up the hood, I used the other to unlatch the prop bar and hooked it into the underside of the hood. Now I wouldn't have to worry about it dropping and decapitating me while I filled the engine with oil.

When I was finished, I reversed the process and brought the hood to within a few inches of the latch and then let its own weight drop the hood into place, being sure to pull my fingers out at the last minute. I'd like to keep all ten. I'd need them for the home renovation.

A free air pump stood near the side of the gas station, and I knew it was in my own best interest to check the tires while I was here and fill them if I could. Arnold meowed from his carrier, obviously not happy about this prolonged detour.

After discovering that two of my tires were low and filling them, I drove over to the pumps and pulled in behind a shiny black pickup. Its owner must be vigilant about washing the winter road salt off of it. Everyone else's vehicles were still covered in the grimy gray film from the New England winter's snowstorms, including my Buick.

I flipped the gas pump mechanism up to hold the trigger

and walked around to open the passenger door. "Hey, buddy, I'm going in to check out the junk food isle while I pay for the gas, if I see kitty treats, they're yours."

Fine. Leave me. Abandon the helpless cat trapped in a box.

"Oh, shush. I'll be right back."

THE GAS STATION'S shop resembled a corner store with its shelves of junk food and chips and refrigerators full of colorful juices and sodas. The place wasn't busy, so I walked up and down the salty food aisle, then walked down the candy aisle. Nothing screamed out to me that I wanted to eat. I really needed a meal, not snack foods.

"Can't find anything?" came a male voice a little too close to my left ear, if I was being honest. I turned to see an older guy with a slight paunch in a biker jacket. I gave him a polite half-smile. "No. I think I'm just hungry for lunch."

"Too bad there aren't sandwiches or something. I could use something like that, too." He grinned at me a little too long. Which wiped the smile off my face in a hurry. It was time to leave. I paid the cashier for a bottle of water and made my way back to the car. Happy to be rid of leering-guy.

I screwed on the gas cap, closed the door, and got into the car.

Kitty treats? I'd really like some after being left all alone in this hot car.

"It's like 40 degrees outside. It's not hot in here."

I thought we were going to eat.

"The only thing they have in there is the perpetually rotating hotdogs."

Oh, can I have one? I can smell them from here.

I put the car into gear. "Exactly why I'm not eating one and neither are you."

Just as I was about to pull out, the black pickup truck cut me off as it raced down the street.

"Jerk." The driver was the lecherous guy from the shop. "Figures."

I pulled out onto the highway in search of sustenance, and I hoped to leave that guy in my dust.

2

After another twenty minutes on the road, I spotted a rest stop that had a food court.

"Here we go, buddy, actual food. Well, sort of."

I need to use the sandbox.

"We can take care of that too, and I'll hunt down some kitty treats for you out of the back."

We made our way down the exit ramp into the rest area parking lot. Immediately, I noticed the black pickup truck.

"Ugh."

What? No food?

"No. That creepy guy is here."

Hiss at him and then bare your claws. It always works.

"Thanks for the advice. Maybe he'll finish his lunch before we get in there. Let's get your litter box out."

I supposed one positive thing of being able to hear my cat with his entitlement complex was that the trip wouldn't be boring. Another was if I could understand him, it kept me from having to clean out a dirty cat carrier.

The litter box was in a tied-up trash bag in the back foot well. I brought it up to the front and took it out of the bag and put the plastic underneath the box. I unlatched Arnold's carrier and let him out. "There you go, my friend, have at it."

If you don't mind, I would like some privacy.

"No problem. I wasn't planning on staying." I got out of the car quickly and made my way around to the back. I used the key to open the trunk and surveyed my mess of boxes.

Not much to begin a new life. But a start. Searching through the first two boxes, I realized I wasn't going to find his treats here. The last box finally had half a bag of chicken flavored mega-treats. His favorite.

When I opened the driver's door again, I almost passed out. "Whoa."

I have covered it completely in sand. You may remove it now.

"Darn tootin'." Thankfully, I was prepared for this. I took the poop scooper out of its plastic baggie and scooped the offending pile of sand into a bag. "Stay here, I'll be right back after I throw this away and wash my hands."

I dropped the baggie in the trashcan that stood outside the dog walk area and went inside to find the bathrooms. The rest area was especially crowded, and at least two people had cat carriers with them. Odd. It must be travel-with-your-cat-day.

A long line snaked out of the women's restroom. Luckily, I was able to squeeze between two women to an unoccupied sink. I washed my hands quickly and headed for the car. Arnold could hang by my side while I ate lunch. I didn't like the idea of him sitting inside the car for that long, even if it wasn't hot out.

"Hop back inside the carrier," I told him. "Let's get some food."

No. I am not going back inside the box.

"Arnold, I don't want to leave you out here alone."

I refuse to be caged again.

"I have your bag of kitty treats." I shook the bag, and he perked up like he had forgotten everything except the sound of treats in a crinkling bag. "Besides, there are other cats inside, you might meet a new friend."

Treats? Can I have them all?

"No. But I'll give you some if you get back in the carrier."

His golden kitty eyes glazed over. *I love you.* He nuzzled the hand that held the treat bag.

"Yes, I know, whenever I hold the treat bag you love me. Get in the carrier." I threw four treats inside and he followed them into the carrier. I locked the door after he pulled his very fluffy tail inside.

He turned and realized he was trapped. *I hate you,* he hissed.

"Yes, I know. Let's get some lunch." I picked up his carrier, and he meowed plaintively.

The weather was still cold enough to know that New England hadn't yet been released from the strong grip of winter, but I wondered if Pennsylvania was slowly waking up into an early spring.

With that thought, a hungry stomach, and an angry cat, I entered the food court.

THE STOP for oil and gas had set me back. This trip was already going to be a long eight hours. I needed to scarf down some lunch and get back on the road.

I stood in line at the pizza kiosk and Arnold complained again about being jostled.

You could be gentler.

"Sorry, buddy."

After receiving my double slices of cheese pizza, I looked out on the sea of tables and located one that was empty and made a bee line for it. Again, Arnold complained with a deep growling meow.

Once I sat down, I realized the table next to us also had a cat in a carrier.

I leaned across the table in the direction of the middle-aged woman that sat nearby and asked, "Is there something special going on? I don't think I've seen this many cats at a rest area before."

The woman turned and smiled. "Yes, there's a Northeast regional competition outside of Philadelphia this weekend." She pointed to Arnold's carrier. "Are you taking part in it?"

"No, no, this is just my pet." I patted the carrier. Arnold meowed in disgust. I wasn't about to translate. "I'm moving to Pennsylvania. I just bought a house down there."

The woman nodded. A green headband held back her shoulder-length brown hair, her earrings were stylized silver cats. "After this past winter, I can understand the need to move south."

I wasn't about to explain that weather had nothing to do with my plans on moving south, so I simply nodded and agreed with her. One thing I could count on in New England—you could always use the weather for small talk.

"We're hoping to get there before this evening. It's the only cat show for Russian Blues this year and we want to be rested and prepared."

"It's a long drive for sure." We both dove into our lunches. The pizza was mediocre but filling, and that's all I needed right now. Arnold was taking a particular interest in the neighboring cat.

A few more minutes went by and Arnold and the other cat continued to mew to each other. I could only get a general idea of what they said, and I had a feeling it was the cat version of flirting. The other kitty was an elegant Russian Blue. They continued their chat until our neighbor finished her meal and got up to leave.

"Have a good drive."

"You too, and good luck at your event."

I watched as she made her way through the crowd to the restroom. We'd have to make a stop there too, before we got back into the car. Arnold's litter box was only for him, as he has frequently informed me. I recalled the one time our neighbor in Stoneport needed a cat sitter, and Arnold steadfastly refused to share his litter box. Before we had realized the issue there were quite a few accidents that had to be cleaned up. Now that we could communicate, I might remind him how we couldn't get the smell out of Darla's favorite rug, and thanks to him we had to throw it out. Fresh start. Now that I've come to understand Arnold, he'll at least clue me in as to why he does what he does.

A meow emanated from Arnold's carrier.

"Keep your fur on, I'm finishing up."

I just had the most amazing conversation. Her name is Oksana.

"Is that right?" I grinned. My beloved pain-in-the-furry-butt cat had a crush.

We have everything in common. She wants to share territory together. He pressed himself against the door of the carrier eagerly.

"That was fast. What happened to dating?" I tried to imagine their commonalities and what Arnold believed "everything" was, if it came to shared experiences or simply avenues of thought, like "all humans are to be used as furniture."

Cats don't do the silly things that humans do; we're cats.

"Of course, what was I thinking? I should know better." I popped the last bite of pizza in my mouth and stood to dust off any crumbs.

I picked up his carrier and grabbed my empty paper plate. People around us stared. Great, they think I'm crazier than the average cat lady for having a conversation with my cat. I took a deep breath. This is exactly why I wanted distance from my sister's lifestyle. I wanted to be normal.

I made my way out of the maze of tables toward the trash cans near the rest rooms. "We need to get going. I'm sorry we're parting ways with your kitty girlfriend."

I told her we would meet her at her cat show later today.

"We don't have time for that. We're meeting the realtor tonight." People stared at me.

Great. I looked like the crazy cat lady talking to her cat. Who was I kidding? I *was* the crazy cat lady talking to her cat.

THE BATHROOM LINE was shorter now, and it took me no time at all to get in and do what I needed to do. I parked Arnold under the sink while I washed my hands and tried to ignore his disdain at being exposed to a 'dirty human sandbox.' His tune changed when Oksana's carrier plopped down next to him. I nodded to the winters-are-too-hard-in-New-England woman who said, "traveling with cats isn't easy is it?"

I rinsed my hands, smiled, and picked up Arnold's carrier while he loudly complained. "She is NOT your girlfriend. Shush." The woman's smile turned to a concerned frown. She snatched up her carrier and left the sinks without drying her hands.

"Now look at what you've done. Everyone here thinks I'm insane." I hissed at him.

I TOOK my time at the hand dryer and tried to regain my composure.

Time to get back on the road. I ignored Arnold, who was trying to convince me to drive him to the cat show.

Just outside the restroom door, I panned the mini mart kiosk to make sure there wasn't anything we needed for the rest of the trip. We'd have to stop for gas again, but hopefully nothing else. Arnold meowed loudly, and another cat answered—Oksana's human was standing in line at the kiosk, gum in hand, cat carrier on the ground next to her.

The apprehensive look on the woman's face was enough to dissuade me from even thinking about any prospective purchases. Arnold had different ideas. I was so frustrated. "Enough, Arnold! I'm not buying something so you can talk to your girlfriend." I clapped a hand over my mouth.

My face burned red. I closed my eyes for a second and gathered my thoughts. I am not like my sister; I will not be the crazy one. I do not hear cat's voices in my head.

Deep breath in, deep breath out.

I opened them to see the sleazy guy from the gas station walking toward me. Seeing him jolted me out of my embarrassment. In his hand he held a cat carrier. He focused on the lines to the kiosk. In one fluid motion, he swapped out the carrier that held Oksana with the one he had been carrying. He continued walking past as if nothing had happened. I had to blink to believe what I had seen. It happened so fast.

"Hey!" I shouted at him. He walked faster but didn't run

or call attention to himself. He wove through the maze of tables like a pro.

The cat's owner turned to me, in fact, everyone in the line turned to me. "Someone just stole your cat." She stared at me confused, then inspected her cat carrier. "No, they haven't. She's right here." She eyed me with suspicion, picked up her cat carrier, as if *I* were the suspicious one, and tossed her gum back onto the shelf.

"But that man. He stole your cat." And he was getting away. I scanned the crowds. He was nowhere. Already gone.

The woman I had met was quickly making her way around the tables to the exit. I followed her. "I saw a man swap out your carrier with a different cat."

The woman picked up the carrier and looked at it, closely peering inside at her cat. What she thought was her cat. "She's right here. No one stole my cat." She spoke slowly, like she was talking to a child. We were now out on the sidewalk next to the parking lot. I scanned the area and found him. I pointed at the black pickup truck as it peeled out of the lot and headed for the highway. "There he goes."

The woman ignored me. She shoved her cat carrier inside her car, glanced back at me one last time, and quickly got into her car.

3

Before I thought it through, I hopped into the Buick and quickly buckled Arnold into the passenger seat. We sped out of the parking lot in pursuit of the sleazy guy in the pickup truck. Back on the highway, heading south, I had a relatively clear view of all four lanes. A number of truckers trundled along, which impeded the view, but I could have sworn I spotted the black pickup ahead. I leaned a little harder on the gas pedal. The temperature gauge shot up. In her geriatric state, Babs was not meant for speed. I eased off the pedal but tried to keep my focus up ahead so I could follow the cat-napper.

"I'm not crazy. Sleazy guy stole that cat."

Arnold had been meowing a sad lament since the kiosk.

My dear, sweet Oksana.

"We'll get her buddy. I promise." I kept an eye on the truck as it weaved through traffic. My Buick would never be as nimble as his pickup truck, especially at the speed he was going. But for now, I could see the highway to the horizon, and I would do my best to keep an eye on him.

He wove in between tractor-trailer trucks and cut off

unsuspecting cars, all while harboring the cat carrier, bungeed securely in the truck bed. All at a speed I couldn't maintain.

A tractor-trailer truck for a large grocery chain, with a photograph of grapes, apples, and strawberries on its side panel, edged alongside me, blocking my view. I moved out of the middle lane over to the left passing lane, with the intent to speed up, ever so slightly, and pass the big rig. But the road was downhill, and the tractor trailer had more momentum. No matter how hard I tried, when I inched forward a little, the trailer would gain on me. I was forced to hold back because I didn't want the Buick's engine to overheat.

Finally, I accepted defeat and sat back on the gas enough to fall at the rear of the tractor-trailer. I eased in behind him in the middle lane. Then traffic increased and a number of slower moving cars pinned us behind the truck. I couldn't move into either lane, now. Frustrated, I kept an eye on my rear-view mirror for a break in traffic as it drove around us.

Why do we have to stay in these lanes, can't we just hop on top and chase after the evildoer?

"One, a car won't jump, and two, it's a rule that we have to stay in the lanes."

Who makes up all these rules?

A car in the right-hand lane had passed me and I moved over. Finally, a clear view of the highway.

I spotted the pickup truck in the distance, driving more sedately than when he first got on the highway. He was far enough ahead that I wasn't sure if we'd ever catch up to him.

As the highway cut into the horizon, I watched as the pickup truck disappeared.

"Crap."

What?

"I can't see him anymore."

You can't see him? Listen and smell! Listen and smell! Arnold turned around and around in his carrier. Then he began to scratch at the sides.

"Buddy, I can't do either of those things to find him." An idea came to me. Watching the road, I took out my cell and called 311. The police information line.

I had often been with my sister when she made calls like this. After she had "seen" something. Something that might help the police stop a crime or solve a mystery of some sort. So, I knew how to handle myself, but still, doing this felt awkward.

"Local Police. How can I help you?" A woman answered.

I cleared my throat. "I'd like to report a stolen cat."

"Are you the owner?"

"No, I witnessed it."

"Have you spoken to the owner?"

"Yes, but they didn't believe me that their cat has been stolen. Because the guy swapped it out with a look-alike cat."

"We would need the owner of the animal to place the request for assistance." Her voice let me know she thought I was insane, too.

"Stealing an animal is a crime, right?"

"Yes. But can you prove that the cat was stolen?"

"How can I prove the cat was stolen?" I looked at Arnold, I looked at the phone, I looked at Arnold again. I hung up.

"How am I supposed to tell the police why I know that the owner has a look-alike cat? 'Oh yes, officer, it's because my cat talked to her cat. He has a crush on her. The cat in the crate is not the same because my cat told me so.'"

"This." I shook the phone. "This is why you and my

sister are so frustrating. I hate this whole psychic mumbo-jumbo stuff." I stuffed the phoned back in the cup holder.

ARNOLD LICKED HIS PAW, *Call Darla, she'll know what to do.*

"I know what to do. *I* do. We're going to tail this guy until he stops somewhere." We did not need to call Darla. Or explain to the police how my cat can verify the identity of his girlfriend-cat.

The bottleneck of tractor-trailers had cleared, and we were now cruising on a long downslope. I could see an enormous expanse of the highway in front of us. The truck was a tiny black dot far ahead. I had to find a way to catch up to him.

I laid on the gas a bit more to see just how far I could push the car's acceleration. I was happy to see that I could keep it at a consistent speed, where it wouldn't heat up. But any faster than that and the temperature light would blink on. Still, I felt like we might be gaining on our culprit.

The tiny black dot got larger.

"I can see them up ahead, Arnold. We'll get them."

An hour passed, my hands gripping tight to the steering wheel.

A dark blue SUV passed me on the right. A light brown minivan passed me on the left. The minivan's windows were covered in adages for a cheer team. "Go team!" and "Cheer!" Along with drawings of a megaphone and pom-poms in blue and white. The blue SUV pulled up alongside them. The boys in the SUV were trying to get the attention of the girls in the minivan. I just hoped someone kept their eyes on the road.

Ahead of them was the black dot of the creepy guy's pickup truck. I couldn't exactly tell if I was slowly gaining on him, but at least I could still see him up ahead. We hadn't lost yet.

We were heading toward the New York bridges, and I hoped that our thief was not going into the city. We were still on I-95. Heading into the city meant more traffic, but fewer tolls. Easier on my bank account, but it might be harder to follow him.

AS WE APPROACHED THE CITY, traffic came to a crawl. The bridge traffic was slow, but I could still make out the black dot that marked our creep. Poor Oksana was in the back of that pickup truck with all the noise and exhaust from a multitude of vehicles. My anger at this guy was growing and my foot got heavier on the pedal as we exited the bridge. The congestion of cars cleared up. I had to remind myself that if I pushed the car too hard, we'd end up on the side of the road without any hope of tailing our bad guy.

Traffic began to move again, and I pushed the car to go as fast as it could without the warning light blinking at me.

This trip was the longest Arnold had ever been on, and I knew how much he disliked being inside that carrier.

"How are you doing, Arnold?"

I am plotting the ways in which I plan to eviscerate this cat-napper.

My voice went up an octave, and I raised my eyebrows. "Good to know. I'm glad you're on my side."

"Meow."

I wasn't quite sure how to interpret that. But I had a feeling he was hinting that things could always change. I shook my head. Crazy cat.

Up ahead our cheer team opened their window and

shook a pom-pom at the SUV. The SUV then rolled down their window and waved a soda can.

I tried to calculate which lane would be the better option if those two vehicles decided to cause a massive collision on the highway. I moved into the middle lane, keeping my eyes trained on the black pickup in the distance. Limited to sixty-five miles an hour, I still held a small spark of hope that we would catch him.

A large tractor-trailer was approaching me from the right-hand lane. As they got closer, I realized the large stacked truck held huge trimmed logs.

"That's something you don't see every day."

Because of the amount of traffic, the group of us moved along the highway like a caravan. Some vehicles pulling ahead, some dropping back. But the same cars together. Traffic was heavy, but steady. I could still see the black pickup truck far ahead. I took a swig of water from my water bottle and jammed it back into the cup holder.

In my rear-view I witnessed a large tractor-trailer as it came barreling down the left-hand lane.

"I'm pretty sure that's illegal, pal." Yes, I talked to fellow drivers who couldn't hear me.

What's illegal?

"Tractor-trailers passing in the left-hand lane. I'm pretty sure it's illegal in New Jersey. Most states actually."

The speeding tractor-trailer whizzed by. Aptly, the side panel was a photo of a huge beer bottle tipped to look like a rocket taking off.

I snickered. "Ha."

Suddenly, something hit my windshield, and I jammed on the brakes. A pom-pom flew up my windshield and launched over the cars behind me. My heart raced. The two tractor-trailers on either side of me swerved.

Horns honked farther back; my guess was that the pom-pom landed, causing more problems behind us.

The tractor-trailer trucks evened out, and I brought my Buick back up to speed. But not as fast as my racing heart. Hands shaking, I took another swig of water.

"That was exciting." I breathed out.

Let's not ever do that again.

I couldn't agree more. When I gained enough composure to continue our pursuit of Oksana's kidnapper, I had to wait until we passed a bend in the highway. When I looked out, I didn't see him. Not a single black pickup truck between us and the horizon.

What? I heard you sigh.

"I think we've lost him again." My racing heart sank.

I took a deep breath; we were going to be on I-95 for a while. Maybe there was still hope.

4

It was another hour before we saw the truck again. Reflexively, I gripped the steering wheel. "I see him."

Where? Arnold scratched inside his carrier.

"Up ahead. Oh, I think he's... Yep, he's taking the rest area ramp."

He's preparing to relieve himself?

"Yes, and to tell you the truth, I've chugged so much water I desperately need to use the facilities."

Unfortunately, I too am in need of the sandbox.

"First, we have to catch up to him. If he's too quick, it's possible that he uses the rest area and leaves before we even get there." My foot pressed on the gas a little more, and the temperature gauge rose as well. Exasperated, I eased off. Nothing was going right today. Of course, my phone began to ring.

I glanced down at the screen. It was my sister.

Is that Darla?

"How do you know that it's Darla? What are you, the psychic, now?"

No, I heard you sigh. You always sigh when Darla calls.

The phone rang again. I answered it to make it stop.

"I told you not to call me."

"Do you hate me?"

"No Dar, I just need to be out on my own. It's long overdue."

"You're serious about trying to flip that house?" She accentuated the words, *that house*, as if it were some kind of accident.

"Spare me your psychic-enriched advice. All those things you *feel* about the situation. I don't want to hear it."

"Fine, I won't say a thing. But will you at least call me once you get there, so I know you arrived safely."

"Won't your psychic spidey sense tell you?"

"I just want you to call, okay?"

"Okay. I'll call you but only if you promise, no telling me how to live my life."

"You don't want any advice, whatsoever?"

"No. It's my life, I'm doing it my way. I don't want a single sentence of psychic advice." I paused for effect. "Or I won't call."

A Cadillac cut me off and then jammed on its brakes. I practically stood on mine.

"Look, I have to go. I'm in the middle of traffic, and I just have to go."

"Fine. Don't forget to call."

I pushed the end button.

THE CADILLAC SLOWED to a crawl in the right-hand lane. I was only a quarter of a mile away from the exit. There was no way I could force Babs to speed up and around the caddy and make it off the exit safely. I had to wait it out.

An eternity later, we finally approached the rest area

ramp and pulled off into the parking lot. This rest area wasn't as busy as the previous one. There were only two other cars besides the black pickup, which was thankfully still there.

I wasn't sure what I was going to say or do when I faced this guy. I didn't even know his name.

The police weren't helpful, and the owner didn't even have a clue. Suddenly, the whole prospect of confronting this guy made no sense whatsoever. I told Arnold as much.

You will rescue Oksana for me. I know you will, because you are my human and you do everything for me.

"Thanks for the vote of confidence, Your Highness."

Pulling into a spot next to the pickup, I rolled down the windows a crack, put the car in park and turned off the engine. "I have an idea. Stay here. I'm going to try to steal Oksana." I unbuckled my seatbelt.

Excellent.

Out of habit, I grabbed my cell phone and jammed it in my back pocket, took the keys and stuffed them in my front pocket and closed the driver side door. I looked around; no one. I ran to the pickup truck. The cat carrier sat in the front driver side corner of the truck bed with a slew of bungee cords crisscrossing it to hold it against the cab.

"Hey there, Oksana," I whispered. "I'm going to get you out of here." I grabbed one of the bungee cords and tugged on it. It snapped back and hit the inside of my wrist. Pain exploded up my arm. My fingers on that hand went numb. I worked on the next bungee cord as fast as I could. And then the next. That's when I heard footsteps.

"Hey, what are you doing? Get away from there."

Frantically, I worked at the last remaining bungee cord when a large hand closed over mine. I tried to yank free, but his grip was like iron. I turned toward him.

"Oh, it's you." He grinned. "You're that sweet thing I met at the gas station."

His sour breath hit my nose, and a wave of nausea rolled through me. I wanted to grab the cat and run. But when the only other person at the rest area got into their car and drove off, I realized we were out of luck.

I shouted, "I'm taking back the cat you stole."

"Who says I stole it? This is my cat." He slyly grinned.

"I watched you steal her." She meowed. Agreeing with me.

"No, you didn't. You have no proof."

My mouth opened in a rebuttal. Nothing came out. He was right. There was no way for me to prove it. Or at least no way that any sane person would agree with. But I knew it. He knew it. But there wasn't much I could do. He squeezed my wrist.

I released my grip on the carrier's handle. But he tightened his grip on my wrist, anyway.

"You sure you won't stay for some company?"

I yanked my arm, trying to pull it away. "You repulse me."

Anger flashed in his eyes, and he forced a grin on his face. He released my wrist by throwing it to the side. "Get out of here. I have a payment coming to me. Stay out of my way." I stepped back from the pickup truck.

Oksana meowed sorrowfully in her carrier, as he pulled bungee cords across the crate and soundly secured it to the truck bed.

He got behind the wheel and started the truck. He smiled creepily and waved, waggling his fingers in my direction. I jumped back as he jammed his foot on the accelerator, spun out of the parking spot, and gunned back onto the highway. I was so angry; I could barely breathe by the time I got back in my car.

Do you have her?

"No. But now I'm fuming mad. And more determined than ever to make that guy pay." I jammed the key into the ignition, I had to come up with a plan. I turned the key, and nothing happened. The Buick simply sat there.

"Are you kidding me?" I yelled at Babs, how could she let me down like this? I closed my eyes and took a deep breath. Slowly, I turned the key again. Nothing.

Now what? I let my head rest on the steering wheel. I took a deep breath. "Good news, we have time to use the restroom."

ARNOLD USED his litter box first, while I stood outside the car, somewhat patiently. I hopped from foot to foot and tried not to think of running water while I waited for him to finish. After the litter was cleaned up again, I eased him back into his carrier. "I'll be quick. Then we can try again."

I'll need kitty treats and some water when you return.

"Will do." I locked and closed the door and headed into the building. The place was empty and quiet. I was grateful I didn't have to wait in any line because now I really had to go. When I came back out, I stared at the vending machines. I was torn between Skittles and a Snickers bar and finally settled on a Cow Tales, a long roll of caramel with a sugar cream filling. I needed all the decadence I could get.

The caramel and sugar cream melted on my tongue. I took a deep breath. The weather was cold but, looking up at the sky, the clouds didn't look like snow or rain. I counted my blessings. I walked back to the car and hopped inside, grateful for the warmth.

"Okay, buddy, out you come." I pinched the spring-loaded lock on his carrier, and he leapt out of the box into the footwell.

He turned and put his paws up on the passenger seat and stretched. His back arched like a gymnast.

That carrier is much too confining. Treats, please?

I gave him a few. "Take it easy on those or you'll run out before we even get to Pennsylvania."

They don't sell these everywhere?

"No, they do not. So snack accordingly." I savored the last of my caramel and settled into the seat. I should try to start the car again and see if the engine would turn over. Delaying the inevitable, I asked Arnold what else he needed.

I would like some water, please.

I cracked open my water bottle and poured some into a small dish. He lapped the water greedily.

I hate this dish. It cramps my whiskers.

"I'll unpack your bowls when we get to the house. Right now, we need to focus on getting there."

I spent more time than I needed cleaning up after Arnold; his spilled water, snack crumbs, and litter that he had kicked all over the floor. When I couldn't delay any longer, I put the key in the ignition and said a silent prayer. I turned the key.

Nothing.

What next?

We were going to have to call a tow truck.

With surprise, I noticed my phone still had 75% charge. I never remember to charge it. I thanked the universe for small favors and dialed a nearby tow company.

"Hey, yeah, I'm at a rest stop off Route 95 and I need a jump. My car won't start."

"We can send someone in an hour." The woman's voice sounded like she was busy and bored.

"Really? Nothing sooner?"

"Sorry."

"Okay, I'll be here." I gave her the specifics, ended the call, and leaned back in the seat. "Well, Arnold, we'll be here for a while."

An hour can be very short if one has enough treats.

"No dice buddy, the treats have to last you until we get to Pennsylvania, and we have at least another 2 hours once we hit the state line."

I lifted my water bottle to my mouth and took a swig. "That guy will be able to get far ahead of us now. We'll never catch him."

My poor Oksana. Arnold moaned.

"The guy hadn't mentioned the cat show. But he must be headed there. Either he is meeting someone there to sell the cat to, or he plans to show the cat to win some money. Those are the only things I can think of."

Oksana is one-of-a-kind. I can understand his desire to possess her.

"Sorry, buddy, I don't think you're going to be able to rescue her. I just don't see how."

Where is this cat show?

We had an hour to wait. I might as well browse the Internet. I put "Russian Blue cat shows" in the browser search bar and watched the results pop up.

"There's a cat show in the Philadelphia area. It's generally on our way to the new house." New house was a relative term, as it was new to me, but hadn't been new in over one hundred and fifty years.

I continued to open tabs and scanned the details of the show. "I think I found it."

Where is she?

"If he's headed to the Russian Blue Regional Cat Show, he's going to Oaks, Pennsylvania, a suburb of Philadelphia. Which is on our way, if I make a detour."

You would make a detour for me?

"Of course, for you. And for Oksana. That poor cat has no idea what's going on, and that guy is a real dirt bag. But there're no guarantees that is where he's heading, and I don't see how we can catch up to him in time."

I glanced up at the rear-view mirror as a tow truck pulled off the highway into the rest stop.

"Okay, buddy, back in the carrier. Once this guy shows up, I'm not talking to you." I needed this guy to help with Babs. I didn't want to give him any reason to run away.

Traitor.

5

I had sworn off men, so, of course, it was no surprise that the guy walking toward me checked off every box in my list of hot guy requirements.

"Howdy. I got a call your car won't start?" His dark blond hair was longer in the front and short and neat on the sides and back.

"Yes." I got out of the car with a quick glance at Arnold's carrier. "When I turn the key, nothing happens."

"Would you mind if I try?" He pointed to the driver's seat.

I looked up into a set of dark green eyes and had to remind myself to talk. "No, sure, go ahead." I waved at him to take my place.

He turned the key, and the car hummed and clicked but didn't turn over. "Could be the alternator, as old as this baby is, or it could be the battery." He reached down and popped the hood. "When was the last time you replaced the battery?"

I looked up at the sky, like somehow it would know because I certainly didn't.

He smiled. "Right. Let's take a look."

He stepped out of the driver's seat and walked around to the front of the car. He released the catch and pushed the hood up like it weighed nothing. "She's built to last. That is one heavy hood." He propped up the hood's resting bar. "You don't see many of these girls on the road anymore."

Out of his back pocket, he pulled out a credit card sized box with red and black wires. He tested the battery.

"Dead."

I cringed. Car batteries weren't cheap.

"You can't just jump it for me?"

He turned and looked at me sympathetically. "I could jump it and if we got it to hold enough of a charge to start the car, as soon as you turned the engine off, it would be dead again."

I closed my eyes and cursed my ex for stealing all my savings. And I was mad at Darla for warning me not to date him... because that just forced my hand. And mad at myself for dating him anyway. Now I barely had enough money to feed myself and Arnold. How was I going to buy a car battery?

"You really can't jump it, huh?" I looked remorsefully at the dusty, corroded battery.

"How far are you traveling?"

"I'm heading to Pennsylvania."

He shook his head. "You'd have to stop at some point between here and there, wouldn't you?"

I shrugged. He was right.

"I've got a battery in the truck. I can have you back on the road in less than 20 minutes."

"Yeah," I reluctantly agreed. "Alright." This would have to go on my credit card, and I'd have to find a job near Pleasant Pond, like ASAP when I got there.

He went back to his truck and returned with a wrench, a shiny new battery, and a pair of nitrile gloves.

"What's in Pennsylvania?" He asked.

"I'm starting over." I announced proudly. "I'm flipping a house there."

He grinned. "Starting over is good. Sometimes all we need is a fresh start."

"Yeah, I'm tight on cash and I don't know how much I'm going to need to put into the house in order to flip it. I'm hoping I can find a job once I get there."

"Cash flow definitely helps with the stress level; I'll tell you that."

"Stress. Ha, ha. I could do with a little less of that lately."

"Are you in a rush to get down there?"

"Kind-of. I witnessed a guy steal somebody's cat at one of the rest areas up north. I'm trying to get the cat back to the owner." I thought of this and wondered how it could possibly happen. There were a lot of unknowns with my plan. I instinctively glanced into the car and knew I would do it, anyway. Arnold was counting on me to at least try.

He turned to stare at me. "Seriously?"

"Yeah, and when I told the owner, she didn't believe me because the guy replaced the cat carrier with a look-alike."

"No kidding?"

"Unfortunately, I met the guy at an earlier rest stop, a total sleaze. When I saw him again, he was stealing a cat. The last thing I wanted to do was follow him."

"Hey, if someone took my dog, I would move mountains to get her back."

I grinned. He was definitely my kind of guy. "My cat is in the front seat." I pointed to the passenger door. "He's my best bud. I couldn't imagine if someone took him from me.

That's why I ended up following this guy. It hasn't been easy; Babs doesn't like to go above sixty-five."

He snickered. "The old girls usually don't. So, I guess you lost his trail at this point, right?"

"I don't know how we could possibly catch up to him now."

"I might be able to help with that."

"How? I don't even know what's going to happen if I finally catch the guy. I mean, I caught up to him here at this rest stop, and there was no one to help me out. He simply took my hand off the carrier, pushed me away, and drove off."

"Have you called animal control or the police?"

"I tried the police. They were kind of skeptical when I mentioned that the guy swapped out the carrier for a different one that was identical. It didn't help matters when I mentioned that the owner didn't believe me. I guess they wanted a call from the actual owner."

"Well, I think the owner will be very happy to hear that you have found their cat. No matter what happens. I would be." His smiled melted the icy cold knife in my heart that my ex had left behind. A little.

He put the new battery into the car and attached the red wire and then the black one.

"We should be able to start her up now. Do you want to give it a try?"

I nodded, walked over to the driver's side, and sat down. A quick turn of the key and the engine roared. "The car sounds brand new. Well, almost."

He chuckled.

I pulled out my phone case and retrieved my credit card from the back of it. "Here you go." I handed him the card.

He didn't reach for it, but smiled again. "Don't worry about it. Think of this as my good deed for the day."

"Car batteries aren't like five bucks. Here, take it." I pushed my credit card in his direction.

"I'm serious. I got it covered. You're doing a good deed for someone who doesn't even know it. Now, let me see what I can do to help you with that. Do you have his license plate number?"

"I remember some of it." I told him what I could remember and watched as he picked up his CB. He talked for a bit and when he came back, he grinned from ear to ear.

"I got you covered. That guy won't be going fast anytime soon, at least not while he stays on the interstate."

"What did you do?"

"I made sure that he has some problems passing a few truckers."

"You're kidding?" I smiled.

"Good luck confronting the guy. Make sure you have witnesses. I hope you get the cat back. For its sake and the owner's."

"Thanks. Is there any way I can thank you?"

"Just be safe and get that cat back. It's no problem." He turned and walked back to his truck.

I couldn't let him just disappear. "Hey, um, do you have a card or something?"

He turned and grinned. I wished I hadn't sworn off *all* men. He unbuttoned the pocket on his chest and took out a business card and handed it to me. "Here ya go, just in case you need it."

"I'll give you a call." I can't believe I said that. My face lit up with embarrassment. I turned away quickly and got back into my car. Before I closed the door, I shouted, "Thank you!"

I looked down at the card. His name was Wyatt Holland. "Thanks, Wyatt."

6

Can the box on wheels move now?

"Yes, buddy, we can get on our way thanks to Mr. Holland."

Are you going to share your territory with him?

"What?" Flustered, I fumbled with the keys. "No. Geez Arnold, is that all you think about?"

Yes. Can we continue our rescue of my dear Oksana?

"You can also thank Wyatt for that too. Hopefully, our cat-napper will be detained by his truck driving friends."

We will catch him.

"We can try."

I put the car in gear, backed out of the parking space and put my foot on the accelerator to put us on the highway. Wishing Wyatt could have magically made Babs go faster as well. But he had definitely done the next best thing by finding a way to slow down our cat-napper.

We drove for a short while when the map on my phone told me the next exit was onto I-78, towards Pleasant Pond. Decision time. I could stop all this nonsense and get on with my new life and turn onto the road that would take me straight to my new town. Or I could continue to follow I-95 with only the slightest hope that I would catch up to and rescue Oksana from the bad guy. And even then, I would still need to figure out some way to reunite the kitty with her family.

I thought about it for a minute and came to the same conclusion Wyatt had. That, if she were my pet, I would be desperate to get her back. Sure, Arnold is snarky and talks back. He's picky about his food and doesn't always appreciate when I pet him, or do anything for him, come to think about it. But he's my best friend, my buddy, and I'd be lost without him. I wasn't sure if this kitty's family felt the same, but she deserved the chance to be with her own family and not with someone who stole her for cash.

I watched as the exit ramp passed us by and we stayed on I-95. I made a quick call to the realtor, postponing our meeting at the house until the next day. I would have to pay for a hotel room tonight instead of sleeping in my new house. I physically cringed at the thought.

Wyatt had reminded me I was doing the right thing. And hopefully his friends will be able to help by keeping this guy occupied until I could get another chance at cornering him and getting Oksana back. I was no longer alone in this. I needed more witnesses this time around. Someone to keep this guy from driving off with Oksana.

A consistent speed of sixty-five miles per hour kept the Buick's temperature down and allowed us to continue our slow charge toward our criminal.

We continued on I-95 and I hoped the guy didn't take a detour. With some luck, he'd drive straight to the cat show. If he had other intentions, we were sunk.

Arnold and I chugged along through central New Jersey when I saw them.

Three tractor trailer trucks huddled together on the highway in the right and middle lanes, like a triangle. This had to be Wyatt's friends. No self-respecting truck driver would go thirty miles an hour on the highway unless they were headed uphill in a snowstorm. They were creating quite the problem—a traffic-jam bubble. Cars honked and drivers rolled down their windows to swear.

I edged my car closer behind the single truck in the middle lane. Sure enough, a black pickup truck with a cat carrier bungeed against the cab was pinned in the right-hand lane. Poor Oksana. The truck looked tiny compared to the two eighteen-wheelers flanking it. Without someone to call off the dogs, these trucks would keep him penned up. I grinned.

And then I realized there really was no way to call them off. I didn't know how to communicate with the truckers to tell them that I was here now, I could follow this guy, as long as he didn't go over sixty-five miles per hour.

I decided I should be content with following him at thirty miles per hour for the foreseeable future. If the drivers released him from the trucker induced slowness, he'd probably speed like a maniac.

I settled in behind the outside truck. But I stayed back far enough that our friend wouldn't notice my Buick was a part of this little group. If he knew I continued to follow him, he might try something evasive. I needed him to believe he was free of me. For now.

He wasn't going anywhere, or so I thought.

The truck in front of me backed off a bit, and I tapped my brakes. Space opened for the guy. He could easily move into the middle lane. The black pickup lurched forward to take advantage of the space.

The trailer sped up to cut him off, and his red lights

flashed as he stomped on the brakes. Oksana's carrier wobbled but held securely to the cab of the truck. Had he secured it properly after our last meeting? I stared at the truck bed and willed the bungees to be strong.

The truckers toyed with him. I imagined them laughing together over the radio. Sleazy guy and his truck settled into their confinement for the time being.

It didn't take long before we crossed over the Delaware River into Pennsylvania. And soon afterward we exited onto route 276 toward Oaks, PA. Thank goodness. Confirmation that he was headed to the cat show. Twenty minutes later, he peeled off the highway and onto the exit toward Oaks, leaving the truckers behind. I followed him at a distance. I hoped he continued to focus on the road in front of him, because there wasn't much traffic for Babs to hide behind.

When he pulled into the driveway of a hotel chain, I continued straight and turned into a gas station. We had him.

I sat in the quiet car for a moment. "Well, I can't confront him in the parking lot, alone."

You're not alone. You have me.

"Arnold, you can't, you're not..." I stopped that train of thought, Arnold wanted to protect me. I couldn't tell him he wasn't enough. "Thanks, buddy. But besides a bodyguard, I need witnesses."

I filled the Buick's gas tank. Both of us needed a bathroom break, and dinner wasn't such a bad idea either. I looked at my phone; it was 7:30 p.m. Next step was to get into the hotel and keep an eye on Mr. Catnapper.

I pulled the Buick around to the back of the parking lot. My big beauty of a car happened to be highly conspicuous. I couldn't hide her behind the little blue Echo in the parking lot. I drove to the middle of the lot and found an SUV that fit the bill. I pulled in, parked the car, and eased myself lower into the seat so just my eyes peeked over the window ledge.

What's going on? I can't see.

"He's getting out of the truck. He's unhooking the bungee cords from around the carrier and taking Oksana into the hotel front door."

We must follow him.

"If we follow him, he'll see us and he'll either run or he'll threaten me. We need to be more judicious about where we confront him with Oksana. There needs to be people around."

Arnold raked his claws against the inside of the plastic carrier. *Let me out of this box! I'll show him who's boss.*

"I don't doubt it, buddy, but that guy is bigger than you. No offense, but I'd like to keep you in one piece. We just have to have a plan."

ONCE THE GUY entered the hotel, I sat up and took a sip from my water bottle, realized it was empty, and put it back in the cup holder. My throat was parched. "We're going to have to go in eventually."

What are we waiting for? Let me at him.

"We're waiting for him to check-in. If we go in now, he'll see us and, as they say, the jig is up. We need to be stealthy. You're a cat; you should know these things."

What I know is that we should be in there slicing and dicing this guy and taking Oksana back.

Mental note to self: keep Arnold in his carrier so he doesn't run off and do something we'll both regret later.

"Okay, so here's the plan. We're going to go in like we're a part of the cat show. Obviously, this hotel allows pets. You just have to pretend you're a Russian Blue."

I am a fastidiously groomed domestic long-haired black cat with impeccable markings.

"Yes. You're fabulous, you're just not a Russian Blue. So, you'll need to hide in your cage... and get hissy if anyone tries to look inside." I wasn't sure anyone would care, but I wanted to cover our bases.

That I can do.

"He should be finished checking in by now. Ready?"

I got out of the car. The evening air was cold with a humidity that sent a chill up my spine. I opened the back seat, grabbing my overnight bag, which I had planned on using tonight when I first got to my new house. I stuffed my disappointment down that this detour was delaying my new adventure. I dragged my bag around to the passenger side and retrieved Arnold.

"Let's do this."

"Meow."

I walked briskly across the parking lot to the main entrance of the hotel and stepped inside the lobby. The warm air made my body shiver off the last of the cold. I glanced around quickly and couldn't see our criminal. I didn't have reservations, and I didn't have the money to pay for them. This would have to go on my credit card. After all, I couldn't very well sleep in my car. Although I did contemplate it. One hundred bucks a night was too rich for me. Heck, I couldn't afford fifty bucks.

I approached the counter. The middle-aged woman glanced up from her computer.

"May I help you?" Her voice was slightly more chipper than you'd expect at this hour.

"I'm interested in making a reservation for tonight."

"Oh, I'm terribly sorry. We're full for the night. The cat show is tomorrow, and we're all booked up."

This changed things.

"That puts a monkey wrench in my plan." What could I possibly say to make her keep an eye out for my cat-napper?

"Would you like me to call other hotels? I can see if there are any vacancies?"

This would buy me time. "Sure. Cat-friendly, of course." I lifted my cat carrier, but not high enough that she could see inside. "Do you mind if I wait in the lobby?"

"No, of course not. Please, feel free. We also have a refreshment area down the hall to the right." She waved a well-manicured hand in that direction.

Refreshment sounded wonderful, and it would also give me an opportunity to look around the hotel.

"Thank you." I walked with my suitcase and Arnold in tow. Down the hallway and to the right I found a coffee and tea station.

Are there any kitty treats?

"No buddy, sorry. There might be a few left in the car. Do you want me to get them?"

No. Please. We must keep an eye on our goal. Rescuing Oksana.

I poured myself a cup of hot water and dropped in a tea bag. I sipped it slowly, letting the hot water ease the chill from my bones. Time to think through my next steps.

I was sure they would allow me to sit in the lobby for as long as I wanted. But I definitely wouldn't be allowed to sleep here. The cat show was tomorrow morning. I had a hunch that if he was headed there, we would be able to corner him.

My new life plan was to follow my own hunches and not Darla's. I laughed. My former self would listen to Darla's hunches and then do the opposite. She told me my last boyfriend was no good. Did I listen to her? No.

And I paid a high price for that. Which is why I had finally broken ties and moved out. I needed to make my own decisions.

I juggled my tea, the suitcase, and the cat carrier back toward the lobby and was met by the woman from the front desk. "There's been a cancellation and there is one room left at the conference center. It's considerably more expensive than here, but for the cat show you can't beat its location. If you head over now, you'll be able to secure it. They're expecting you."

"Oh?" I didn't want to leave without making sure our criminal was in for the night.

"The cat show is across the street from the hotel. Actually, there's an indoor bridge. You don't even have to go outside." She smiled happily. I couldn't tell her that there was no way I could afford the considerably more expensive conference hotel's cost.

But I smiled. "Thank you so much for helping. Would you mind if I sat in the lobby for a bit? I am waiting on a friend." I lied. I wanted to make sure our "friend" was staying in for the night and not leaving and taking Oksana with him.

"Of course. As long as you need." She turned on her heel and headed to the office behind the desk.

I sat on the lobby's couch placing Arnold on the end table. The table stood high enough he could look out. I positioned myself toward the front door. I wasn't sure what else to do. It was late and my body was exhausted, and my brain didn't want to think up any more plans.

I hoped to see the owner of Oksana come walking in the door. Or, if the bad guy decided to leave, my back would be to him as he exited the lobby, and I would see him if he left.

None of this happened. We sat for an hour and no one arrived, and our guy didn't leave. I sipped my tea slowly.

When a woman walked into the lobby, I startled awake and realized I must have been dozing. Arnold meowed.

"Are you here for the cat show, too?" She raised her cat carrier slightly, to a very disgruntled "meow" from inside.

My best bet was to pretend to be one of them. "Yes. But there's no room at the inn. So, I'm waiting for a friend of mine, to let her know I'll be going to another hotel." I impressed myself with how easily that lie tumbled across my lips. Arnold meowed. I focused on my human conversation, so I wouldn't get distracted by hearing Arnold's thoughts in my head.

"Oh, that's too bad. We reserved the hotel as soon as we registered for the show."

"Ours was a spur-of-the-moment decision." Which was actually true. I tapped my hand on top of Arnold's carrier. "I suppose at this late hour my friend is probably already settled. Unfortunately, I let my phone die, so I can't give her a call." That held some truth; my phone was practically dead. I had forgotten to charge it after the tow truck incident. Again, the ease of which I lied to this perfectly nice woman amazed me. I made for a pretty good spy.

"You can use my phone. My name is Marie, by the way." She held out her phone.

"Nice to meet you. I'm Mira. Thanks, but I need to leave for the conference center, anyway." Another truth. Bed was calling. It had been such a long day.

"Well, good luck tomorrow. Don't forget registration is at eight o'clock sharp. You don't want to miss that." She grinned and glanced toward Arnold's carrier.

"No. I don't want to miss that."

"Maybe we'll see you there?"

"I'll watch for you. Good luck tomorrow."

The woman turned and walked over to the front desk. After she got her key card and disappeared down the hallway. I decided it was time for us to find some sort of dinner. The crumbs in the bottom of the corn chip bag in my car were probably not going to make a very fulfilling meal. And Arnold needed a break from his cage. If this guy wasn't coming out of his room for the rest of the night, I needed to make plans for myself and Arnold. Cheap plans.

I stood and touched my toes, or tried to, stretched, and yawned.

We needed some action. I decided I'd get something to snack on from the vending machine.

I glanced over at the desk, but the receptionist was now on the phone and focused on her computer. I crouched down to face Arnold. "How are you doing buddy?"

I understand the need to wait for the appropriate moment before we pounce.

"Do you need to eat or use the litter box?"

I'm in fight mode. The answer is: no.

"I'm going to get a snack from the machine down the hall."

I looked up and noticed the woman was no longer on the phone and our eyes met. She had obviously seen cat owners talk to their pets before. She grinned.

"You wouldn't mind keeping an eye on him while I get something from the vending machine?" Honestly, I was exhausted from the stress of driving so far while tracking a catnapper. I needed a moment to myself to grab some food and figure out my next step.

"Not at all."

I took my phone and its case, which held my cash, what little I had, and walked down the hall. Maybe another cup of tea at the refreshment station. I fed my dollar bill into the vending machine and stared at the selection. Unlike the rest area vending machines, this one held healthier options and toiletries, useful if I ended up sleeping in my car, after all. I opted for the unfrosted strawberry Pop-Tart, wishing it had icing. But I'd settle, as my option was that, or a granola bar. I peered out the side window next to the vending machine. It showed a wide view of the parking lot. The Buick's nose peeked out from behind the SUV. My stomach dropped, as did the pop tart. The pickup truck was gone.

I ran down the hallway, crushing the pop tart in my rush to the lobby. How could I have missed him?

Arnold was still where I left him. I let out a breath. I leaned over his carrier. "He got away. We missed him somehow."

Arnold let out a grumbling whine from deep in his throat. I stood up. We had no idea where he was now.

I let out a quiet moan. I walked over to the entrance. And moaned again.

"Can I help you with anything?" The woman asked tentatively.

I took a deep breath and lied through my teeth. "I think my friend has left. Can you give me the directions to the conference center hotel?"

"Sure." She clicked away at the keys on her computer and printed directions to the hotel. "This should get you there."

I graciously took the pages. With a dead phone, there was no other way to find the conference center. "Thank you. I might as well get ready for tomorrow." I forced a grin on my face and grabbed Arnold's carrier and my suitcase.

"Thanks again for making arrangements for me. I really appreciate your help."

"Not a problem. Have a good evening." She leaned forward to peek at Arnold.

"And good luck to you, tomorrow."

He hissed riotously at her and she jumped back.

"Sorry, I think he's just tired. Thanks, again."

A half-smile wavered on her face as she went back to her computer. We walked out of the hotel and into the cold, dark parking lot.

Once we were out there, and no one would hear us, I asked. "How could we have missed him?"

Maybe he scented us.

"You think he knew we followed him?"

"Meow."

This was a mess. We had spent most of the day following this guy in the hopes of rescuing a poor stolen kitty, only to have him slip away at the end of it all.

Arnold meowed angrily and scratched at the plastic. I'm sure he was wishing it was the bad guy's face. I know I did.

"The only thing we can do now is hope he shows up tomorrow at the cat show." I would see this to the end. We were less than two hours from Pleasant Pond; we had time. I decided we'd splurge. As much as I loved Babs the idea of a soft bed obliterated any thought of spending the night cramped inside the car. After everything that had happened today, Arnold and I deserved a cozy hotel room.

7
_____

We sat in the car. Arnold wanted nothing. No treats, no food, not even a sip of water. He was still in pursuit mode, he told me.

I studied the printout with directions to the conference center. Less than ten minutes away.

My stomach growled. Unlike Arnold, I was no longer in pursuit mode. I was in cranky, hungry, exhausted mode.

I loved the sound of the car revving the first time I turned the key. Again, I thanked Wyatt in my thoughts.

Surprisingly, I managed not to get us lost. Of course, it helped that once we were in the vicinity of the conference center, there were signs everywhere pointing us in the right direction.

It actually cost money to park. I groaned as I took out my credit card and slipped it into the slot at the parking garage attached to the hotel.

"This is one expensive pursuit, Arnold."

We are rescuing a cat in peril.

I grinned. "Yes, I just wish it were cheaper."

I found an empty parking spot on one of the upper

decks. I took out my suitcase and retrieved Arnold from the front seat. The idea of a comfortable bed to lay down in was so appealing for a moment I didn't care how much this hotel room was going to cost me. I was also starving, and wished desperately that I hadn't dropped the Pop-Tarts on the floor, or had gone back for them. But I hadn't, and now I needed to remedy that before I could sleep.

We walked into the hotel lobby with its shiny marble floor and its impressive track lighting. I realized if I got room service, I'd be paying through the nose.

"May I help you?" The perky man behind the desk asked.

I put on my best pretend-you're-a-functional-adult face. "Yes, I was just at this other hotel, and she didn't have any rooms, so she reserved a room for me here."

I lifted Arnold's carrier slightly. "I'm here for the cat show?" I couldn't help the level of uncertainty in my voice. I wasn't sure what I was doing here. I just needed sleep.

"Sure. Let's see." He typed away at the computer. "Yes, here it is, Mira Michaels, for one night." He typed away on the keyboard, grabbed a key card, and put it inside the cardboard wallet and slid it across the counter toward me.

"Your room number is..." He wrote it on the front of the wallet. Not that there was anyone to overhear what my room number was. But still the discretion was appreciated.

"And would you like a chocolate chip cookie? Fresh-baked." He leaned forward with a huge plate of cookies; the scent of warm chocolate enveloped me in chocolaty goodness.

I almost passed out from relief. "Yes, please." I took two. They were warm and soft, and he handed me a paper napkin to lay them on.

"We have a refreshment center by the elevators, with hot coffee, tea, and cocoa."

"Thank you very much." Absolutely, thank you very much. This was going to be my dinner. And that's when I realized I had left Arnold's dinner and litter box in the car.

I would have to do a second trip. I took a deep breath. One thing at a time. I stopped at the refreshment stand and got myself some tea, herbal, so I could sleep. A large bowl of red apples sat at the end of the table. I pocketed two, one for tonight and one for breakfast tomorrow.

"Come on Arnold, let's go see this room of ours." Awkwardly handling the cup of tea, the suitcase, and the carrier, we made our way up to our room. Once inside, I let out a sigh of relief.

It had a soft bed, it was clean, and it was mine for the night.

I leaned my suitcase against the wall, set my tea down on the counter, and placed Arnold's carrier on the floor. When I opened the carrier, he darted out and stretched.

"Don't pee on anything. I can't afford to pay any kind of fee for you if you mess up the carpeting."

He stretched again and let out a long-drawn-out meow.

"I'm going down to get your litter box and your food and water dish. Be good or else."

As I walked down the hallway toward the elevator, I wondered what exactly "or else" could be. *Or else* he doesn't get to sleep on the bed with me. *Or else* he doesn't sleep on the pillow on top of the bed, with me? Arnold was exceedingly spoiled for a cat. But he was my BFF, and on this big adventure, we were in it together.

When I got to the lobby, I decided to explore a bit. I only prayed that with the extra time away Arnold would not cost me an exorbitant amount of money by peeing on the rug.

I went to the front desk and asked, "Can you tell me how to get to the conference center from here? Where I would need to go tomorrow for registration?"

I was still fascinated by how easily the lies kept falling out of my mouth every time I needed them.

Darla would be mortified. She was kind of big on truth telling.

"Sure, if you follow this hallway," he pointed to the right, "down and to the left, you'll see a bridge. It's inside, of course, and goes over the road and into the conference center. Once you get across, there are doors into the conference center itself. It's late right now so I don't think you'll be able to get into the conference center. The doors will close behind you on the bridge, so make sure you have your hotel key card with you."

"THANK YOU." I headed down the hall to the walkway that led to the bridge. I tried the doors on the other side of the walkway—locked. It wasn't the time to explore. The last thing I needed was the possibility of getting trapped in a dark conference center for the night.

I went back to the parking lot and got Arnold his things. The parking garage was full. Tomorrow's cat show would prove one of two things: one, that we were crazy to have followed this guy all the way down here, as I would not be able to find him again, which would end the entire search and rescue, or two, we would be able to find Oksana but not her owner. My mind was a jumble and tired. Those cookies were waiting for me up in the room. I hurried back to the hotel room and put down the water and food for Arnold, which he ate quickly and then used the litter box. Thankfully, I had also remembered the scoop. I flushed the poop, so I didn't have to smell it for the rest of the night. With my luck it would backup the hotel plumbing.

After devouring the cookies and noshing on the apple, I got ready for bed. I brushed my teeth and climbed into the nice soft bed with clean sheets. Then I remembered my dead phone. I had to plug it in.

I got up and rummaged through my bag for the charger. I found it in the bottom corner, crunched up in a ball. I unwound the cord and plugged it into the nightstand lamp, which had a USB on its base. Perks of a pricey hotel.

Before I climbed back into bed, I set an alarm for seven a.m. Just to make sure we could scope out the registration table early enough to catch this bad guy. Then on to the real adventure; my new house.

I snuggled into the pillow and was practically asleep when I felt Arnold's little paws as he stepped daintily across my pillow, curled up beside my face and fell asleep. Tomorrow was another day.

MY ALARM BLARED through my dreams of car chases and cats getting catnapped over and over again. I groped, half asleep, to turn it off. Today was the day. Either we found the bad guy with Oksana or... well, we would find him and that was that. After I showered and gathered everything up, Arnold quickly climbed into the carrier. He wanted to find this guy too. I kept envisioning us finding the guy red-handed and reuniting Oksana with her real owner. It was the only thing I could do to keep me moving forward. I was determined to be successful. Until I looked at my phone. Eight-fifteen.

I had been so tired last night I had screwed up the alarm. Registration had already started.

My cell phone was fully charged for the first time in days, and I wound up the cord and stuffed it in my suitcase. We headed out in the direction of the refreshment stand. I forgot about my breakfast of an apple and a cup of coffee. I didn't bother checking out. I knew the hotel would bill me electronically. I raced down the hallway that led to the bridge and the conference center. My key card was still with my phone, just in case.

The bridge spanned across a small roadway and was walled with windows. I watched as cars came and went as I ran across the silent rectangular space.

I pushed open the doors. The sound of hundreds of people hit me. One glance and it was clear this show was for cats and the people who loved them. Everyone wore cat paraphernalia. Headbands, stickers on their faces, and jewelry with cats on it. Most toted cat carriers and a few pushed cages around on wheeled carts. All of them with a purpose, heading toward the registration area.

I kept an eye out for two people, the sleazy guy I chased across the interstate highways, and the woman with the green headband who was the true owner of Oksana.

I considered looking for a woman with a headband, but realized today she may not be wearing it. I thought I spotted a black leather jacket that the sleazy guy wore. We headed in that direction.

The room was filled with long tables with white tablecloths that skimmed the floor. On each table sat rows of metal cages, decorated to the nines with velvet and glitter and other objects, making each cage unique for its inhabitant cat. Photos of the cats were pinned above the cages. Some even sported brass plaques.

Arnold was speechless with all of this. He hadn't said anything since we entered the conference center. I wondered what was going on in his brain.

I arrived where I had last seen the guy. I turned around, looking. Nothing.

"Can I help you? Oh, hi!" It was Marie from the hotel.

"Marie..." I glanced around hoping to spot sleazy guy.

"Registration is that direction. If you haven't registered your cat yet." She attempted to peek in at Arnold who instinctively hissed at her and she leaned back. "Not in the mood for the show today, are you?" She asked him. "Between you and me, I'm not either."

"It's our first time." I said.

"Well, it's good you're giving it a try."

Maybe she could help me, especially if she was sitting here, she might have seen our bad guy.

"Have you seen a man in a black biker jacket about this tall?" I tried not to make negative comments about him. I might have to say he was a friend of mine or some such nonsense. But I was going to avoid that if possible.

"I haven't. I've been paying more attention to the cats. I'm only showing one cat this year." She turned to speak to a large elderly man wearing a volunteer badge. "Greg, did you see a guy with a black jacket around?"

"Most people check their coats. It gets hot in the main area. I did notice a man in a jacket. Maybe that direction." He pointed around the corner.

"Thanks, Greg. Thanks, Marie. I appreciate it."

"Good luck, today," she said, a bit despondently. My sister would make it a point to find the reason why and attempt to help, but my sister wasn't here today, just me. I was so close to the end; I needed to stay focused.

· · ·

How was I going to find Oksana in the maze of tables?

Oksana's owner should be here, too. I scanned the crowd for both the man in the leather jacket and the woman's face that I had only seen once, and even then, for a very short time.

When I got to the third row of tables with cages and meowing cats, I saw a woman looking very confused and upset. She had the right color hair with a blue headband that had cat ears on it. I walked up to her as she was putting the Oksana doppelganger into a cage. "Are you the woman I met at the rest area? I told you someone took your cat?"

She angrily bolted the door of the cat cage and looked up and recognized me. "Oh, my gosh." She pulled me into a hug. "I should have listened to you. You were right. This is not my cat. Poor Oksana. And I think we could have won! This sweet thing is not my cat." She gestured at the lovely Russian Blue sitting regally in the cage in front of us.

"I think the guy that took your cat is somewhere at this event. But I'll need your help to find him."

"He's here? Oksana is here? I'll do anything to get her back! I'm Elaine."

"Don't worry, we'll find her. I'm Mira." We didn't bother shaking hands, besides carrying a suitcase and a cat carrier, I was on a mission.

Arnold meowed and caught my attention.

Don't you dare even think of leaving me trapped in here. I will be the one to rescue my sweetheart.

I didn't think taking him out of his carrier was a good idea, but I didn't want him to freak out either. He could create quite the racket, when he wanted to. Other owners walked around with their docile cats. I supposed it didn't matter anymore if people noticed that he wasn't a Russian

Blue, since we were already inside the conference center. "Only if you swear not to run, I'll carry you with me."

Done.

"Can I leave these at your table?" I pointed to my suitcase and carrier.

"Of course." She lifted the table skirt. "Under here."

I shoved my suitcase under her table where it couldn't be seen. Against my better judgment, I took Arnold out of his carrier and pushed the carrier under the table as well. Arnold put his front paws on my shoulder to look around.

"You stay put, buddy." Lots of cat people talk to their cats, this time I fit right in. It was only me that could hear them talk back.

Elaine seemed surprised at my non-show worthy cat. "Okay, let's go." She and I marched up and down the aisles looking for our bad guy. Surprisingly, a moment later, I spotted him stuffing his face with a donut at the refreshment table.

"That's him," I shouted, which was the worst thing I could have done, because he turned towards us. He recognized me mid-donut bite.

I ran to him, juggling Arnold on my shoulder, who leapt off and onto the bad guy's face.

The guy screamed like a banshee, so loud and high-pitched that I wanted to put my fingers in my ears. Instead, I peeled Arnold off of him.

"Tell us where she is." I demanded. I wrestled Arnold under control. But that didn't mean I wouldn't let him loose again if the guy didn't answer me.

"Where have you taken my Oksana?" The owner demanded.

"I don't know what you're talking about." He glanced to the right, giving away his lie.

"She's over there, isn't she?" I pointed.

He began to stammer as he stood up. "No, no, I don't know what you are talking about."

Enough was enough. This guy had toyed with all of us and all our cats too long.

"Go ahead, Arnold." I released my puffball of claws as a distraction and dashed over to the tables at the right. His screams followed me as I pulled the fabric table skirts up on every table and upended empty cat carriers hidden beneath. People yelled at me as I frantically searched for Oksana.

Under the last table in the row, I knocked into a cat carrier which wouldn't budge. Jackpot. I pulled it from under the table.

"WHAT'S GOING ON HERE?" A gruff voice sounded over my shoulder. I straightened up, triumphant, to find a uniformed security guard right behind me.

"She sicced her attack cat on me!"

"He stole my cat!" Elaine bellowed.

"I found Oksana! Arnold. Get over here!"

Arnold untangled his claws from the leather jacket and the man's face and ran to meow at the cat carrier in my arms.

"Oksana!" Elaine opened the carrier and examined her cat.

"IS THIS TRUE?" The security guard addressed us all at once. I didn't know whether he was asking if I had sicced my cat on the guy or if the guy had catnapped Oksana, but both were actually true.

"Yes." Elaine and I said in unison.

"No. No, I have no idea what these crazy women are talking about." Again, he was such a bad liar even the security guard gave him the side eye.

"Do I need to check the chip inside the cat to verify ownership?"

"She's chipped. Go ahead and check." Elaine pulled Oksana from the carrier and cradled her like a baby. "You're okay. My dear one."

"Look, it wasn't my idea." The catnapper put his hands up in the air in defeat. "It was hers." He pointed to a woman grooming a cat at the table I had just pulled Oksana out from under. "I didn't want nothing to do with it."

"What are you talking about? I don't know this man!" She stuffed her cat back into its cage.

"You lie. You old hag. You paid me to steal this cat so you could 'double the odds' you said."

I picked Arnold up to my shoulder so he could peer lovingly at Oksana.

"I would like to press charges on this man for stealing my cat."

"You'll need to come with me." The security guard took the man by the elbow. "Once things have settled down, please come by the security station and give your statement."

The man yanked his arm away. "I can walk on my own." Over his shoulder, to the woman, he yelled, "I'm going to make sure they arrest you, too."

The old woman looked at the cat-napper through a slitted eye. She quickly packed up her belongings, including her cat. The owner and I watched as the woman left the conference hall.

"If she's registered and had anything to do with it, the police will be able to find her."

I hoped she was right. Nothing was worse than tracking down someone. I now knew from experience.

8

"Oksana is a titled cat. That woman has been our closest competitor for years. Only Oksana stood between her and a first-place ribbon."

"And I suppose she decided to do whatever it took to get that win. Including stealing Oksana. But why bring Oksana here?"

"Probably to show both cats and double the chances of winning."

Arnold mewed endearingly at Oksana. Oksana purred loudly in return.

I explained to the woman how I had followed the man all the way here from Connecticut because I was sure that Arnold would want to see Oksana back with her original owner. "My cat meowed sadly the entire way. I couldn't just let the catnapper get away with it."

She was taken with how sweetly the two cats got along.

When we arrived at her table, we realized we had a problem on our hands. A third cat, with no owner.

"What do we do about this poor cat?" I pointed to the look-alike kitty that currently sat in Oksana's cage.

"She's probably chipped like Oksana. We can take her up to the registration desk and I believe they can scan her chip there. We'll be able to find out who the owner is," Elaine said.

I made a mental note to get Arnold chipped. It had been really helpful today.

The owner put Oksana on the table, opened the cage, and took out the lost kitty. She placed Oksana in the cage instead, and Arnold jumped down to join her.

I gave him an exasperated look. "You should be back in your carrier. This is Oksana's."

"We'll only be a minute; he can stay. Look how sweet they are." The cats nuzzled each other and murmured sweet nothings. I refused to translate Arnold's private thoughts. Nobody needed to hear that fluff. We walked to the registration table with our poor kitty. "We found a missing cat."

"No problem. We can scan her and get her back with her owner in no time." The woman took out a scanner and after a few beeps along the cat's neck area, a name popped up.

I wondered what the chances are that this cat, who had been stolen because she looked like Oksana, had an owner who was here at this cat show. Maybe my ride wasn't over. Maybe I'd have to return another cat to its proper owner before this day's adventure was done. I only had a few hours before my appointment with the realtor at my new house. Even thinking those words, 'my new house,' gave me a thrill.

"Marie Salsberry." And before either of us could say anything, the registrar turned on the mic and announced. "Marie Salsberry, we have located your cat. Please see us at the registration desk to claim her."

Sure enough, it was the same Marie. As soon as she saw the cat sitting demurely on the registration desk, she leapt forward. "How? How did she get here? My Sissy, I've been worried sick! I thought you ran away from home."

"Unfortunately, she was taken by that man as a decoy." I pointed in the direction of the security guard who was holding the leather-jacket guy in custody.

She glared at him. "That's my neighbor, Frank. He's awful. I'm not surprised in the least. I hope he gets jail time. In fact, can I press charges?" The registration lady shrugged her shoulders. Clearly that was outside her jurisdiction.

Marie cuddled her fur-baby and turned to me. "Thank you so much for finding my cat. How could I possibly repay you?"

Elaine interrupted, "I can pay for your hotel reservations from last night. For finding my dear Oksana."

Marie wasn't to be outdone. "I can buy you lunch and pay for your ticket fee for entering the cat show. You will stay?"

I hadn't considered staying. "Unfortunately, I need to get back on the road. I have an appointment in a few hours."

"Well, maybe next time. Here's my card and twenty dollars for your lunch. And thank you so much." Marie held onto her cat, Sissy, and walked back to her table.

"I'll need to get Oksana ready for judging. But come back to my table with me and I'll phone the hotel. You said you stayed here at the conference center?"

"Yes, I did. And I really appreciate that you want to pay for the hotel room."

"It's the very least I could do."

We arrived back at the table. Both Arnold and Oksana were sitting next to each other ever so sweetly in the cage. Arnold had his paw on top of hers.

"Oh, my goodness, they're so adorable." Elaine beamed. She took out her cell phone and called the conference center hotel. Once that was completed, I thanked her again. And she thanked me again. "I wouldn't have my Oksana back and she is my favorite kitty." As if on cue, Oksana meowed.

"Let's get you brushed out and ready for the judging."

"I wish I could stay. But my appointment is about two hours from here." At least, thanks to Wyatt Holland, I knew my car would start.

"Have a safe journey." She reached over and hugged me. "Here's my card. I breed Russian Blues, if you're ever interested in a kitten."

I smiled. "This one is more than a handful." We both laughed. "Good luck with the competition."

"I actually think Oksana is going to miss your dear kitty. What's her name?"

"She's a he: Arnold."

She gave a startled look. "Oh," She looked a bit concerned but then smiled. "Have a safe trip."

I waved back as I pulled my suitcase and carried Arnold out of the conference hall. We were done with the cat show. I was able to get back on the road again. This time without the chase scenes.

We walked back through the bridge and through the hotel to get to the parking garage. After all the excitement, I was ready to finish this drive. I was ready to start my new adventure.

"Come on, Arnold, let's get back on the road. Let's get to our new home."

He didn't respond. Which surprised me. But when I leaned over and peered into his carrier, I noticed that he was sleeping soundly, making little tiny kitty snores.

"I guess running in hot pursuit-mode wore the little guy out." I whispered.

I used my phone as a GPS again and easily found the highway. Pleasant Pond was a short hour and twenty-five minutes away. And then our new adventure would begin, one without car chases and over the top drama. I voted for no drama whatsoever. Just nice, quiet, small-town living.

A SNEAK PEEK OF KEYS AND CATASTROPHES

The Sunday morning light warmed the inside of the car as I turned off the highway onto the exit ramp. The long road trip was about to come to an end. A worn wooden sign with flecking white paint announced that we were in Pleasant Pond, Pennsylvania, the town I planned to call home. At least for the time being.

"Meow." Arnold wanted my attention again. *May I remind you that I did not willingly agree to this whole experiment?*

Curls of hair fell out of my ponytail. I tugged on the elastic and ran my fingers through it quickly. Juggling the steering wheel, I pulled my hair away from my face and up into a tighter ponytail. I took a deep breath.

Again, against my better judgment, I answered him. "We've already talked about this. I understand you don't want to move to a new house."

The next meow sounded more like a rumble in his throat. *I miss Darla.*

"I get it that you love Darla, but she micromanages my life. I really don't want to talk about it anymore."

Arnold's thoughts were in my mind, as clear as if he were talking to me. I had given up trying to ignore it. Because as much as I didn't want to be anything like my psychic sister, communicating with my cat had its upsides. Like company on this long car ride or reminding him to use the litter box and not the inside of the carrier when he got mad at me.

And I'd like to remind you that I am completely over riding in this locked box.

"You have to stay in the carrier because they have rules about animals in cars."

He circled inside his carrier. *Whoever made that rule was obviously not a cat.*

"It's for your own safety." I had another mile to go before we would be on the outskirts of town.

I would like to take a break.

"I can stop up ahead and give you more treats. Let me focus on driving and not panicking, okay? Aren't you supposed to provide emotional support?"

I am not required in any way to be an emotional support animal.

"I get it, buddy. You are king. I am your human. Now let me drive."

I felt like a lunatic when I talked to Arnold. But I had spent too many months ignoring his voice in my head. It made life simpler to just listen and respond. It definitely helped with all the territorial peeing and scratching. Not me —the cat.

After the last big blow-up with my sister, I found a list of "Best Places to Live in America" and closed my eyes and poked a finger at the computer screen. I chose Pleasant Pond, Pennsylvania. I figured a town with such a name would be a great place to start a new life. After that, I searched the real estate pages. That's when I saw it. This gorgeous Victorian on the cheap. Like very cheap. Of course, there was a catch, I thought, *there is always a catch*.

I was adventurous, but I wasn't dumb. Three months ago, when my money was still safely in the bank and not in the hands of my no-good ex, I flew down and checked out the place before I bought it. When I saw it for the first time, I had been pleasantly surprised. It was a tall, somewhat narrow Victorian with all the eye-catching extras. It reminded me of fairy tales and secrets. Truth be told, it needed work. But not as much as I had expected. As soon as I walked through the door, I had the feeling that Arnold and I needed to be there.

The realtor, Rebecca Branson, seemed edgy throughout the house tour. When we got back to her office and settled in at her desk, I asked. "So, why is it so cheap?" I didn't mention that cheap was a relative term. Rebecca, with her manicured beach-vacation-blue nails and perfectly styled hair, wouldn't look me in the eyes.

Obviously prepared for the question, she recited her response. "The town owns the house and wants to see the main street revitalized. Because this house has some issues, they've dropped the price to make it more appealing to buyers who are interested in fixer-uppers."

I nodded. I'd seen it before. Cities, but usually large cities, offering up townhomes for a dollar with the stipulation that a certain amount of money was to be put into rejuvenating the residence. Only this contract didn't require me to put any money into the place. The house was just cheap. Which was also the only reason I bought it.

After purchasing the house and thanks to my very ex-boyfriend, I only had a tiny bit left over to start the process of flipping the house, and that was assuming I ate Ramen and learned how to plant a vegetable garden.

I gave her a questioning glance.

She leaned closer. "I'm not supposed to tell you, but you might as well know. The place is haunted."

A laugh burst out of my mouth. The absurdity of it all hit me like a water balloon. Of course, it was haunted, because the universe thought it was one big joke that I could never get away from the legacy of my family. The realtor probably assumed I was laughing for other reasons. Disbelief maybe. Still, I laughed.

But she didn't even grin. Instead, she frowned at the unsigned paperwork.

"The town wants the house sold." She shoved the paperwork back in its manila folder. "I shouldn't have said anything."

"It won't keep me from buying it." My sister was the one who dealt with ghosts, not me. "I don't believe in ghosts," I lied.

She tucked a lock of her blond hair behind her ear. "You still want to go through with the sale?"

"I need to start somewhere." Now I would have a house with its own history, its own story. This was not exactly what I was looking for, but it would have to do.

She shrugged. "Okay." She pulled the paperwork back out of its folder and cautiously pushed it across the desk to me. She watched me sign *Mira Michaels* and her whole body visibly relaxed. "I used to think the same thing until I started working in that house."

Curiosity had me. "Really?"

She involuntarily shivered and she slipped the done deal back into its folder. "I'm happy to have it off my list, finally."

"Wow. That bad?" My stomach tightened. *What had I just*

done? But the thought passed quickly. I had to get out from under my sister's thumb. Whatever happened, I would deal with it.

She nodded slightly and caught herself. "Goodness, now you don't want it."

"On the contrary."

"Well, then, welcome to Pleasant Pond, and please, call me Becca."

I gathered up my copies of the papers, shook her hand, and left. I was getting away from my family and proving to myself I could be an adult on my own, my sister didn't need to mother me. Haunted house or not.

Now I had returned with all my worldly possessions and Arnold crammed into my ancient Buick. Its peeling paint would fit right in with the exterior of my future home. The fact that I had sunk every last penny I owned into the house was not an exaggeration, and the reality of it made me short of breath. I could live a few months on the money still in my bank account, but I would definitely need a job. The realization of it all, that I was on my own, sink or swim, hit me.

My heart pounded. My vision blurred. I pulled off to the side of the road and parked the car.

Breathe in, breathe out.

I had to prove to myself and my sister that I didn't need her constant input in my life to survive.

Arnold meowed from the carrier. "Sorry, buddy. I just needed a breather." Arnold was the one cat that didn't puke when in the car. He didn't enjoy car rides, but he wasn't hyperventilating either. That was me. Breathe in, breathe out.

What if I couldn't make the money I needed? Worse, what if I somehow managed to do all the work and pay for it and couldn't find a buyer? Well, I would figure it out. One step at a time. That's all I could do. I wished Arnold *was* an emotional support cat. I could use some words of comfort in my head right now.

My car shook as someone drove by at a speed quite a bit more than the recommended speed limit. I glanced in my rearview but only saw the dust the car stirred up, and police lights. It wasn't until the police officer knocked on my window that I realized he wasn't pulling over the speeder that just flew by, but me.

Really? My heart rate tripled. If I got a ticket, whatever money I had would be gone. Why was he pulling me over?

I rolled down my window. The officer wore plainclothes.

"Is there a problem, officer?" I was still in the middle of something resembling a panic attack, and my breathing came in hitched and uncomfortable breaths.

He peered in and cleared his throat. "I pulled you over because one of your taillights is out."

Of course, he was good looking because that's what happens when you swear off all men. "Correction, I pulled myself over because I was having a panic attack. And you're not helping." My anger at the universe now got heaped on to this guy.

He examined me closer. "Do you need assistance? Are you okay?"

"What kind of question is that? Of course, I'm okay." I was not having a panic attack, I refused. I was handling this move just fine. Lying to myself came in quite handy at the moment.

"If you need assistance, I can have an EMT out here."

"How bad do I look?" I glared at him. I put my hand up. "Don't answer that." I hadn't slept well in two days and I had a feeling it showed on my face.

"If you don't need any assistance, you are free to go. But get that taillight fixed." He rested his hand on the open frame of the window, tapped it and stood back.

"Why are you giving me grief? Why don't you pull that speeder over instead of giving a girl a bigger panic attack for arriving in town?"

He paused for a moment. "Sorry about that. I'm Detective Lockheart. Welcome to Pleasant Pond." His eyes looked me over, again. "Are you sure you're okay to drive?"

"I'm fine." I snapped.

A frown creased his face. "Get the taillight fixed." He turned and strode back to his car.

A deep breath in didn't calm me down. I closed my eyes. When I opened them my rearview showed the police car still sitting there. I took another breath. I hoped this guy didn't work in this town, but knowing my luck...

"We best get going, huh, Arnold?"

His lack of response meant he was more than done with this little journey of ours. I just hoped he'd be okay with the change. Maybe this old house will have lots of mice for him to chase.

I put the car in drive and pulled back onto the road. I amended my thought—I'd rather have ghosts than mice.

WE CONTINUED our adventure into our new town. I drove down Main Street per the stated twenty miles per hour speed limit. I certainly could not afford a ticket.

The town center was compact and small. The bank and post office shared a low, squat tan brick building. The grocery store looked more like a house on the corner. Almost every other storefront was dark and empty, with

"For Lease" signs in the windows. At the end of the street stood a brightly painted diner called Soup and Scoop. My stomach growled. The clock on the dash read 11:30. I wasn't meeting Rebecca until 12:30 when she'd hand me the keys and do a final welcome walk-through. There was still time for a bite. I pulled into the small lot in back of the Soup and Scoop.

"Sorry, Arnie. I'll be quick, I promise."

A low rumble from the carrier.

"I know, I know. I swear I'll let you out as soon as we get to our new home, you'll love it."

Hopefully, the Soup and Scoop had cat-friendly policies and they would let me bring him inside. If not, I'd have to rely on takeout. Although the idea of me handling soup in the car or at the new house without furniture was not something I could see happening without some drama.

I dropped a couple of Arnold's favorite treats into his carrier. His black nose turned away, and he licked the long ebony colored fur on the underside of his paw. If anything, Arnold kept his fur as neat as Hercule Poirot's mustache.

I grabbed his carrier and walked around to the front of the diner. In direct contrast to the storefronts along Main Street, which looked empty and vacant, the diner's exterior was a chic combination of sky blue and teal with shining chrome accents. The bell on the door rang as I pushed it open and walked into the diner's wonderfully ethereal yet comforting vibe. The light blue sparkled Formica tables, white checkered floor, and additional chrome accents made me feel instantly welcome.

I stood there with the cat carrier, not daring to step farther in with a cat in hand. Of course, Arnold picked this moment to be completely silent and not help me get the attention of the waitress at the back of the room. Her dark blond hair was pulled up in a ponytail and she wore a classic 50's diner apron. But she must have heard the bell because she turned to us and waved for me to wait. She finished the order for a cute guy with dark hair and a short beard. He was the only one in the place, and I sincerely hoped he lived in town. For him, I'd give up my thoughts of avoiding relationships. The waitress came over, smiling.

"Hi there, how can I help you?" Her ponytail bobbed.

"Table for one?" I looked down at the floor by the door. "Can I bring my cat in here? I didn't want to leave him in the car."

"I totally understand. You can take him to your booth with you."

"Really?"

"I own the place. And my brother is the only one here now. I don't think he'll mind." She waved a welcoming hand toward the booth near the door.

Arnold meowed. I decided it best not to translate my hyper-privileged cat's response.

"Thanks. I appreciate it. Arnold appreciates it too." I gave the carrier a slight nudge to remind him of his manners.

She crouched down to peer into the carrier, her gray eyes bright and cheerful. "Hey there, little guy, I bet you're ready to get out of that box." She stood and pulled out a menu from behind the napkin dispenser. "Here you go, and if you have any questions, just let me know. I'll be at the counter making a shake."

"Will do." I hoped the food was good because if it were, I could see myself here often. Then I checked reality and realized I had very little, if any, expendable cash to splurge on eating out.

I pushed Arnold's carrier into the booth so it faced me,

even though he would clearly let me know if he needed anything. "It's okay, buddy, I'll make this fast. I promise."

He settled his head on his paws to wait it out. *Be quick about it.* Patience wasn't his strong suit.

The blue vinyl booth was cozy; the Formica table with its chrome trim was adorable. Reading the menu, I grinned. Soups, sandwiches, and ice cream.

The soup of the day was handwritten on the menu—squash bisque—which sounded perfect. It even came in a bread bowl. Awesome. I opted for a milkshake, chocolate malt. Soon after I put the menu on the table, the waitress came back with a glass of water, a cloth napkin, and silverware. "What can I get you?"

"The squash bisque sounds great, and can I have that in a bread bowl?"

"Gluten-free or regular?"

"You have gluten-free here?" In a small town, I didn't think they would have gluten-free anything.

"I'm gluten-free myself. I feel like the gluten weighs me down, spiritually."

The spirituality thing reminded me of my sister, but I couldn't help but like this woman's bubbly personality. "Just the regular, and can I get a chocolate malted milkshake?"

"Of course, you can. Oat milk or regular?"

"Regular whole milk."

She smiled just as happily and took my order. "Are you making your way up to the Grand Canyon?"

I wasn't sure what she meant. "Isn't that in Arizona?"

She grinned. "The Pennsylvania Grand Canyon. It's nearby. People stop here on their way out to visit it."

I had never heard of the Pennsylvania Grand Canyon. "Sounds like a great place to visit."

"It is." She wrote everything down on a small white

board. "I'll have Robbie put this right in for you. We don't want your kitty to have to wait too long."

Because this day has already been insufferably long. Arnold grumbled.

"I'm moving in today, just up the street. So, I have cat food. He won't have to wait long at all," I reminded him.

Her eyes lit up. "That's wonderful. We'll be neighbors. I live in the next house over from the restaurant."

"That makes you my first new friend." I felt just as cheesy saying it as it sounded.

"I am Aerie, by the way." She stretched out a hand, and we shook.

"My name is Mira Michaels. Nice to meet you."

"Mira, you have a wonderfully bright aura and it's very nice to meet you too."

I smiled. Yep, serves me right. I exit my relationship with my psychic sister and my first new friend runs along that same vein. Well, not the exact same, I hoped. But her infectious positivity seemed to clear the air, and I didn't mind so much.

Within minutes, Aerie brought me a beautiful bread bowl of soup that smelled of sage and pumpkin squash. The bisque was the best I'd ever tasted. It had just the right amount of sweet and savory, and the bread was so fresh that I couldn't help but dip it into the soup over and over again. I focused so much on my meal I had stopped "listening" for Arnold who meowed to remind me of the real purpose of today, and it wasn't enjoying a bowl of soup.

"Sorry, buddy. I'll finish up," I whispered.

I dabbed my mouth with my napkin and folded it neatly on the table. The cloth napkins gave the restaurant such a homey feel. I asked Aerie for the check, but she interrupted me." Don't worry about it. It's on the house. Welcome to Paradise Pond!" She beamed another smile at me.

"Are you sure? I don't mind paying." I pulled out my phone.

"What are neighbors for? I hope your move goes smoothly. And I hope to see you here again."

"Thanks, Aerie."

I gathered up Arnold, who shifted his weight in the carrier and meowed again. It was time to move in.

Her cute brother looked up from his burger as I was heading out the door. "See ya." He raised a hand and waved. I grinned and waved back. I hoped so.

MORE MIRA MICHAELS MYSTERIES

If you enjoyed this story and would like to read more about Mira and her lovable cat Arnold, check out the rest of the Mira Michaels Mysteries.

Keys and Catastrophes
Pranks and Poison
Construction and Calamity

Please consider writing a review on Amazon to let others know more about Mira's adventures, just don't share spoilers! Reviews help readers find these stories and helps writers like me to continue to write what I love and create more stories for you.

Thanks bunches,

Julia

SUBSCRIBE AND SAVE!

S imply go to Julia's website at
www.juliakoty.com
and click the subscribe button. You'll be included in our exclusive club and be the first to learn about new releases and special deals on the stories you love.

ABOUT THE AUTHOR

Julia Koty is an emerging author of cozy mysteries. This is the first book in the Mira Michaels Mysteries.

Julia spent her early childhood in a small town in Pennsylvania very similar to Pleasant Pond. Her house, also an old Victorian which her dad renovated, was indeed haunted.

Visit her website and subscribe to her newsletter to be a part of the group and learn about exclusive deals on upcoming books in the series.

 facebook.com/JuliaKotyAuthor

Made in the USA
Coppell, TX
02 June 2023

17607034R00059